Maclear & Co.'s Catalogue of Educational Works, English and Classical Text Books, Maps, Charts, Diagrams, & c.

SALZWASSER
VERLAG

Anonymous

Maclear & Co.'s Catalogue of Educational Works, English and Classical Text Books, Maps, Charts, Diagrams, & c.

Reprint of the original.

1st Edition 2023 | ISBN: 978-3-37514-652-8

Verlag (Publisher): Salzwasser Verlag GmbH, Zeilweg 44, 60439 Frankfurt, Deutschland
Vertretungsberechtigt (Authorized to represent): E. Roepke, Zeilweg 44, 60439 Frankfurt, Deutschland
Druck (Print): Books on Demand GmbH, In de Tarpen 42, 22848 Norderstedt, Deutschland

MACLEAR & CO.'S

CATALOGUE

OF

EDUCATIONAL WORKS,

ENGLISH AND CLASSICAL

TEXT BOOKS,

MAPS, CHARTS, DIAGRAMS, &C.

TORONTO:

MACLEAR & COMPANY,

17 & 19 KING STREET EAST,

1858.

SCIENCE AND ART.

		$ Crs.
Bakewell's Philosophical Conversations, ...	E.	... 1 50
Brande's Encyclopedia of Science, Literature and Art, ...	A.	... 4 00
Blair's Why and Because, ...	E.	... 0 30
Brewer's Science of Things Familiar, ...	A.	... 0 62¼
Chamber's Introduction to the Sciences, ...	E.	... 0 30
Child's Guide to Knowledge, ...	A.	... 0 62¼
Fullom's Marvels of Science, ...	E.	... 0 50
Nichol's Book of the Sciences, ...	E.	... 0 45
Peterson's Familiar Science, ...	A.	... 0 75
" " (abridged)	A.	... 0 40
Ure's Dictionary of Arts and Manufactures. 2 Vols.,	A.	... 4 50
Wilson's Catechism of Common Things, ...	E.	... 0 12¼
Youman's Handbook of Household Science, ...	A.	... 1 25

PHYSICAL SCIENCE.

Maury's Physical Geography of the Sea, ...	A.	... 1 50
Smyth's Mediterranean Sea, with Geography of the South of Europe, ...	E.	...
Somerville's Connection of the Physical Sciences, ...	A.	... 0 45
" Physical Geography, ...	A.	... 1 25

TEACHERS MANUALS.

Abbot's Teacher, ...	A.	... 1 00
Northend's Teacher and Parent, ...	A.	... 1 00
Page's Theory and Practice of Teaching, ...	A.	... 1 00
Root's School Amusements, ...	E.	... 1 12¼
School and School Master, by Potter and Emerson,	A.	... 1 00
Symons' School Economy, ...	E.	... 0 88
Young's Infant School Teachers' Manual, ...	E.	... 0 75

MISCELLANEOUS.

Book of Commerce, by Sea and Land, ...	A.	... 0 50
Butler's Analogy, ...	E.	... 0 50
Chamber's Infant Education, ...	E.	... 0 60
" " Treatment, ...	E.	... 0 37¼
" Political Economy, ...	E.	... 0 50
Chevreul on the Law of Colours, ...	E.	... 0 50
Creasy on the English Constitution, ...	A.	... 1 00
Delome on the Constitution, by MacGregor, ...	E	... 1 00
Henry's Shorter Catechism.	E.	... 0 25
Introductory Lessons on the Christian Evidences, ...	E.	... 0 12½
" " British Constitution,	E.	... 0 17
Money Matters, ...	E.	... 0 25

C

MACLEAR & Co. in issuing this Catalogue respectfully ask attention to the following points :

I The absence of any book from the Catalogue must not be taken as proof that it is not in stock, as additions are constantly being made. They will procure a supply of any work immediately there is a demand for it.

II. Any book not in stock they will use every effort to obtain—if American, within a week; and if English, in about five or six weeks.

III, The prices affixed will, they believe, be found as low, and in many cases much lower than those hitherto charged. Occasionally, new editions are issued at lower rates; in such case they will immediately reduce their price. If at any time the price charged is above that marked in the Catalogue, it will arise from the Book supplied being a new edition, which at times are issued improved and enlarged, at a slightly advanced rate.

MACLEAR & CO.'S
CATALOGUE OF EDUCATIONAL WORKS,
&c., &c., &c.

[A signifies American edition.   E signifies English edition.]

GREEK TEXT BOOKS.

		$ Cts.
Anthon's First Greek Lessons,	A. ...	0 75
" Greek Prose Composition,	A. ...	0 75
" New Greek Grammar,	A. ...	0 75
" Greek Prosody and Metre,	A. ...	0 75
" Do. Ed. by Major,	E. ...	0 75
" Jacob's Greek Reader,	A. ...	1 00
" Manual of Greek Antiquities,	A. ...	0 87½
" Do. of Greek Literature,	A. ...	1 00
Arnold's First Greek Book,	E. ...	1 37½
" Do. Key to,	E. ...	0 40
" Second Greek Book, containing an Elementary Treatise on the Greek Particles, and the formation of Greek Derivatives,	E. ...	1 50
" Third Greek Book, cont'g Selections from Xenophon's Cyropædia, with Eng. Notes and a Vocabulary,	E.	0 95
" Fourth Greek Book, containing Xenophon's Anabasis, with English Notes,	E. ...	1 10
" Accidence, with Easy Exercises and Vocabulary,	E ..	1 50
" Practical Introduction to Greek Prose Composition, Part I.,	E. ...	1 50
" Key to do., Ed. by Spencer,	A. ...	0 75
" Do., Part II., containing the Particles,	E. ...	1 75
" Key to do.	E. ...	0 90
" Do., Ed. by Spencer,	A. ...	1 75
" Greek Reading Book,	A. ...	1 25
" Greek Synonyms, from the French of Pillon,	E. ...	1 75
Boise's Exercises in Greek Composition, adapted to the First Book of Xenophon's Anabasis,	A. ...	0 75
Bullion's Greek Grammar,	A. ...	1 00

			$ Cts.
Buttmann's Greek Grammar, ...	A. ...	2 00
Cary's Lexicon to Herodotus, ...	E. ...	1 00
Champlin's Short and Comprehensive Greek Grammar,	A. ...	0 75
Crusius' Homeric Lexicon, Ed. by Arnold, ...	E. ...	2 40
Donaldson's New Cratylus, Contributions towards a more accurate knowledge of the Greek Language, ...	E. ...	5 00
Donnegan's Greek and English Lexicon, ...	E. ...	4 00
Drisler's Greek-English and English-Greek Lexicon,	A. ...	
" Yonge's English-Greek Lexicon, containing all the Greek words used by writers of good authority, in chronological order, ...	A. ...	
Edinburgh Academy. Greek Rudiments, ...	...	1 00
" Greek Delectus, ...	...	1 00
Eton Greek Grammar, ...	...	1 12½
Greek Concordance of the New Testament, with Indices,	A. ...	3 50
Greek New Testament, ...	A. ...	0 75
Do. do. Ed. by Spenser—Maps, Indices, &c.	...	1 00
Hincks' Greek English School Lexicon, ...	E. ...	2 25
Howard's Greek Exercises, ...	E. ...	1 70
Kendrick's Greek Ollendorf, ...	A. ...	1 00
Kühner's Elementary Greek Grammar, translated and revised by Edwards and Taylor, ...	A. ...	1 50
Liddell & Scott's Greek Lexicon, ...	A. ...	5 00
Do. do. abridged, ...	E. ...	2 50
Matthiæs' Greek Grammar, by Kendrick, 2 vols. ...	E. ...	9 00
Novum Testamentum, Græcum, ...	A. ...	0 75
Do. do. Ed. by Spencer, with Maps, Indices, &c.,	A.	1 00
Pinnock's Catechism of Greek Grammar, 2 parts, ...	E. ...	0 40
Pickering's Greek-English Lexicon, ...	E. ...	4 00
Robinson's Greek Lexicon of the New Testament,	A. ...	4 50
Sandford's Introduction to Writing Greek, ...	E. ...	0 80
" Rules and Exercises in Homeric and Attic Greek,	E.	1 35
" Extracts from Greek Authors, ...	E. ...	1 40
Spencer's Greek New Testament, with English Notes, Maps, Indices, &c.	A. ...	1 00
Thiersch's Greek Grammar, ...	E. ...	3 50
Valpy's Greek Delectus, ...	E. ...	1 25
" Elementary Greek Grammar, ...	E. ...	1 75
" " Exercises, ...	E. ...	2 00
Wright's Greek Lexicon, ...	E. ...	1 75

GREEK TEXTS.

Æschines against Ctesiphon, from the Text of Baiter and Sauppe—Notes by Arnold and others, ...	E. ...	1 12½
" Do. Oxford Text, English Notes, ...	E. ...	0 40
" and Demosthenes on the Crown, Oxf'd Pocket Classics,		0 50

						$ Cts.

Æschylus' Tragedies, Oxford Pocket Classics, ... 0 75
" Agamemnon, Oxford Text, with English Notes, E. ... 0 20
" Prometheus Vinctus, do. ... E. ... 0 20
" Persæ, do. ... E. ... 0 20
" Supplices, do. ... E. ... 0 20
" Septem Contra Thebas, do. ... E. ... 0 20
" Choëphorœ, do. ... E. ... 0 20
" Eumenides, do. ... E. ... 0 20
" " revised by J. G. Donaldson, Parker's
       Text, ... E. ... 0 25
Aristophanes—Vols. 1 Selections from the "Clouds," Vol. II.,
       containing the "Birds," 1 with English notes
       and a metrical table, by Prof. Felton. E. ... 2 00
       (Oxford Pocket Classics,) 2 Vols. ... 1 50
Aristotle—Ethica, Oxford Pocket Classics 0 50
Demosthenes—The Olynthiac Orations, English Notes by
       Leland, Doberenz Sauppe, Westermann and
       others. Ed. by Arnold, ... E. ... 0 75
" Orations on the Crown, Edited and Notes as
       above, ... E. ... 1 12½
" Philippic Orations, do. E. ... 1 12½
" On the Crown, Oxford Pocket Classics, ... 0 50
" " Oxford Text, English Notes, E. ... 0 40
" Select Orations, Parker's Text, ... E. ... 0 40
" Adversus Leptinem, do. ... E. ... 0 25
Euripides—Opera Omnia, Oxford Pocket Classics, 3 vols. ... 1 62½
" Tragediœ, Sex. do. 0 87½
" with English Notes, Ed. by Arnold, in 5 vols. Vol.
       1, The Hecuba ; Vol. 2, The Bacchœ ; Vol. 3,
       The Iphigenia in Taurus ; Vol. 4, The Hippo-
       lytus ; Vol. 5, The Medea. The Set, E. ... 5 00
" Hecuba, Oxford Text, English Notes, ... E. ... 0 20
" Phœnissæ, do. do. ... E. ... 0 20
" Hippolytus, do. do. ... E. ... 0 20
" Medea, do. do. ... E. ... 0 20
" Orestes, do. do. ... E. ... 0 20
" " Notes by Edwards, ... E. ... 1 00
" Alcestis, Oxford Text, English Notes, ... E. ... 0 20
" " Notes by Woolsey, ... A. ... 0 75
" Bacchœ, from Bothe, Parker's Text, ... E. ... 0 25
" The Hecuba, Hippolytus, Medea, and Bacchœ—
       English Notes by Anthon, ... A. ...
Herodotus, from the Text of Schweighœuser, with English
       Notes by Wheeler, Ed. by Arnold, Vol. 1, E. ... 0 90
" Oxford Pocket Classics, 2 vols. 1 50

			$ Crs.
Xenophon Anabasis, with English Notes and Grammatical References by Brown. Edited by Arnold,		E.	1 75
Xenophon Anabasis. By Hardy and Adams,		E.	1 25
" " With Notes by Anthon, Map, &c.		A.	1 25
" " " " Ed. by Doran.		E.	2 00
" " " Boise,		A.	1 00
" " Books IV. to VII. with English Notes &c (Arnold's Fourth Greek Book,)		E.	1 10
" Cyropœdia, with English Notes, and a Vocabulary, (Arnold's Third Greek Book)		E.	0 95
" Memorabilia of Socrates, Oxford Pocket Classics			0 35
" " from the Text of Kühner, with Notes by Hickie. Edited by Anthon,		A.	1 00
" " Edited by Robbins,		A.	1 00

LATIN TEXT BOOKS. $ cts.

		$ cts.
Anthon's First Latin Lessons, a Grammar of the Language with Exercises,	A.	0 75
Anthon's Latin Prose Composition,	A.	0 75
Key to do.,	A.	0 50
Anthon's Latin Syntax, with Reading Lessons and Exercises in Double Translation on the basis of Kühner,	A.	0 00
Anthon's Latin Versification,	A.	0 75
Key to do.,	A.	0 50
Anthon's Latin Prosody and Metre,	A.	0 75
" Zumpts Latin Grammar,	A.	0 75
" " " abridged,	A.	0 50
" Latin Dictionary,	A.	2 00
" Riddle and Arnold English-Latin Lexicon,	A.	3 00
Andrew's Latin-English Lexicon,	A.	5 00
Arnold's First Latin Book,	E.	0 80
" " by Harkness,	A.	0 75
" Key to do.,	E.	0 30
" Second Latin Book,	E.	1 00
" Key to do.,	E.	0 55
" Second Latin Book and Reader, by Harkness	A.	0 90
" First and Second Book, by Spencer,	A.	0 75
" Third Book, Word Building,	E.	1 12½
" Prose Composition, Part I.,	E.	1 75
" Key to do.,	E.	0 50
" Prose Composition, Part II.,	E.	2 00
" Key to do.,	E.	0 40
" Prose Composition, edited by Spencer,	A.	1 00
" Verse Composition,	E.	1 50
" Key to do.,	E.	0 55

			$ Cts.
Arnold's First Verse Book, Part I.,	...	E. ...	0 55
" Key to do., ...	...	E. ...	1 00
" First Verse Book, Part II.,	...	E. ...	0 30
" Key to do., ...	...	E. ...	0 55
" Hand Book of Latin Synonyms, ...	...	E. ...	1 12½
" Latin English Lexicon, ...	...	E. ...	2 75
Beza's Novum Testamentum, ...	...	E. ...	1 00
Bohn's Riley's Dictionary of Latin Quotations, &c. ...		E. ...	1 25
Browne's Grammar for Ladies, ...	...	E. ...	0 37½
Bullion's Latin Grammar, ...	...	A. ...	0 87½
Do. do.	...	A. ...	0 75
Carson's Latin Exercises, adapted to Ruddiman,	...	E. ...	0 50
Donaldson's Varronianus, ...	...	E. ...	4 00
Edinburgh Academy Latin Rudiments ...	...	E. ...	0 50
" " Delectus	...	E. ...	0 80
Ellis's English Exercises. Edited by Arnold,	...	E. ...	1 00
Key to do., ...	...	E. ...	0 88
Eton Latin Grammar, Yonge's, ...	...	E. ...	0 62½
" " Accidence, ...	...	E. ...	0 30
" Electa Ex Ovideo, ...	...	E. ...	0 70
Freund's Lexicon. Edited by Andrews, ...	...	A. ...	5 00
Grammatical Exercises adapted to Ruddiman,	...	E. ...	0 50
Harrison's Latin Grammar, ...	...	A. ...	1 00
Harkness' Arnold's First Latin Book, ...	...	A. ...	0 75
" " Second " ...	...	A. ...	0 90
Howard's Introductory Latin Exercises, ...	...	E. ...	0 75
" " " extended, ...		E. ...	1 10
Kaltschmidt's Latin Dictionary, ...	...	A. ...	1 25
Kühner's Latin Grammar, ...	...	A. ...	1 00
McClintock's First Latin Book, ...	...	A. ...	0 75
" Second "	...	A. ...	0 75
Ramshorne's Dictionary of Latin Synonyms,	...	A. ...	1 00
Riddle and Arnold's Latin-English Lexicon,	...	A. ...	3 00
Ruddiman's Rudiments, by Hunter, ...	...	E. ...	0 45
Valpy's Latin Delectus, by White, ...	...	E. ...	0 75
Key to do., ...	...	E. ...	1 10
Valpy's Epitome Sacrae Historie, ...	...	E. ...	0 60

LATIN TEXTS.

Cæsar—Commentaries, Ed. by Spencer, ...	...	A. ...	1 00
" " Oxford Pocket Classics ...	...	...	0 62½
" " Ed. by Bullion, ...	...	A. ...	0 90
" " Ed. by Anthon, ...	...	A. ...	1 00
" " Anthon's Ed. by Wheeler,		E. ...	1 50
" " Chambers' Educational Course,		E. ...	0 75

			$ Cts.
Cæsar—Commentaries, Schmitz & Zumpt,	...	A.	0 75
" " Books I. to IV. f'm Herzog's Text,		E. ...	0 40
Cicero—Select Orations, English Notes, Ed. by Arnold,		E. ...	1 10
" " Notes by Johnson,	...	A. ...	1 00
" " Edited by Bullion,	...	A. ...	1 00
" " Notes by Anthon,	...	A. ...	1 00
" " Anthon's Ed. by Boyd,	...	E. ...	1 25
" " " by Wheeler,		E. ...	1 63
" " Ed. by Ferguson,	...	E. ...	0 40
" " Phillipa Secunda, from Orelli's Text,	... ...	E. ...	0 25
" Tusculan Disputations, Notes by Anthon,	.	A. ...	1 00
" " with English Notes, from the German of Tischer. Ed. by Arnold,		E. ...	1 50
" De Senectute, with English Notes from Sommerbrodt. Ed. by Arnold,	... ...	E. ...	0 70
" " et de Amicitia. Ed. by Anthon,		A. ...	0 75
" " Parker's Text,	... ...	E. ...	0 25
" De Finibus Malorum et Bonorum, with Preface, English Notes, &c., by Dr. Beaven. Ed. by Arnold, ...		E. ...	1 50
" Epistles, with English Notes. Ed. by Arnold,		E. ...	1 37½
" De Officiis, with English Notes, Translated from Zumpt & Bonnell. Ed. by Thatcher,		A. ...	0 90
" " from Zumpt. Parker's Edition,		E. ...	0 55
" De Natura Deorem. Leipsic,	...	...	0 75
" Opera Selecta. Edinburgh Academy,	...		0 88
" De Amicitia et de Senectute. Parker's Text,		E. ...	0 25
" Pro Plancio, from Wunder,	... ...	E. ...	0 25
" Pro Milone, from Orellius,	... ...	E. ...	0 25
" Pro Muræna, ...	... ...	E. ...	0 25
Cornelius Nepos—see Nepos.			
Curtius Quintus, Ed. with English Notes, by Crosby,		A. ...	1 00
Horace, Opera Omnia. Oxford Pocket Classics,	...	...	0 50
" " with English Notes, by Anthon,		A. ...	1 25
" " " Ed. by Boyd,		E. ...	1 88
" " from the text of Orelli, with Notes by Lincoln, ...		A. ...	1 25
" " Notes from Dübner. Ed. by Arnold,	...		1 75
" " Thompson's Edition, illustrated with 250 authentic illustrations, ...		E. ...	1 75
" " Edition by Hunter,	...	E. ...	0 80
" " On the basis of Anthon & McCaul. Ed. by Wheeler, ...		E. ...	2 00
" Carmina. Oxford Text, with English Notes,		...	0 40

				$	Crs.
Horace, Carmina. Parker's Text, ...	E. ...	0	37½
" Satiræ. Oxford Text, with English Notes,	...	0	20
" " Parker's Text, ...	E. ...	0	25
" Ars Poetica, do.	E. ...	0	12½
Justinian, Institutes, with English Notes, Translation, &c., by Sandars, ...	E. ...	4	50
Juvenal, Satires, with English Notes, &c., by Anthon,	A. ...	0	90
" Et Persius. Oxford Pocket Classics, ...	...	0	37½
Livy, History, First and Second Decades, 4 vols. Oxford Pocket Classics, ...	...	1	50
" " Books I. to V., with Notes and Index. Ed. by Gunn, ...	E. ...	1	12½
" Selections from the First Five Books, with Books Twenty-one and Twenty-two entire. Ed. by Lincoln, ...	A. ...	1	00
" " Books I. to V. Ed. by Hickie, ...	E. ...	2	00
Lucretius. De Rerum Natura. Oxford Pocket Classics, ...		0	50
Nepos (Cornelius), with Critical Questions, Exercises, &c. Ed. by Arnold, ...	E. ...	1	00
Key to do.		0	30
" " Oxford Pocket Classics, ...	...	0	35
" " Oxford Text, with English Notes,	...	0	30
" " with Notes, &c., by Anthon, ...	A. ...	1	00
" " with Notes, Index and Vocabulary. Ed. by Stewart, ...	E. ...	0	80
" " Ed. by Bradley, ...	E. ...	1	00
" " Ed. by Valpy, ...	E. ...	0	75
Ovid, Metamorphoses. Ed. by Ferguson, ...	E. ...	0	70
" " Selections from, with Notes. Ed. by Arnold, ...	E. ...	1	25
" " Ed. by Anthon, ...	A. ...		
" Elegaic Poems. Ed. by Arnold, ...	E. ...	0	70
" Fasti. Parker's Text, ...	E. ...	0	50
Phaedrus. Oxford Pocket Classics, ...	E. ...	0	35
" Ed. by Carson, ...	E. ...	0	60
Plautus. Miles Gloriosus. Parker's Text, ...	E. ...	0	25
" Trinnummus, " ...	E. ...	0	25
" Captives. Ed. with Eng. Notes, by Proudfit,	A. ...	0	37½
Sallust. Opera Omnia. Oxford Pocket Classics, ...	...	0	50
" Jugurtha and Catiline, with Notes, Vocabulary, &c., by Butler and Sturgus, ...	A. ...	1	00
" " Ed. by Anthon, ...	A. ...	0	75
" " Notes by Anthon. Ed. by Boyd,	E. ...	1	10
" " Do. Ed. by Hunter,	E. ...	0	60
" Jugurthine War, Notes by Browne. Ed. by Arnold,	E.	0	90

$ Cts.

Sallust.	Jugurthine War, Oxford Text, with English Notes, E.			0 30
"	Cataline, do. do. E.			0 20
Tacitus.	Opera Omnia. Oxford Pocket Classics, 2 vols., E. ...			1 25
"	Annales, with English Notes, translated from Nipperdey. Ed. by Arnold, 2 vols. ... E. ...			2 75
"	with English Notes. Ed. by Tyler, ... A. ...			1 25
"	Germania and Agricola, with Selections from the Annales. Ed. by Anthon, ... A. ...			1 00
"	Germania and Agricola, with E. Notes by Tyler, A.			0 62½
"	Germania, with Ethnological dissertations and Notes, by Latham, ... E. ...			3 50
"	" and 1st Book of Annals. Ed. by Smith, E.			1 37
"	" Parker's Text, ... E. ...			0 25
"	Agricola, do. ... ... E. ...			0 25
Terence.	Comœdiœ, with Eng. Notes, &c. Ed. by Anthon, A.			
"	Andria. Parker's Text, ... E. ...			0 25
"	Adelphi. Do. ... ... E. ...			0 25
Virgil.	Opera Omnia. Oxford Pocket Classics, ...			0 40
"	" Ed. by Cooper, ... A. ...			2 00
"	" Ed. by Duncan, ... E. ...			2 00
"	" Ed. by Thompson, 200 authentic Engravings, ... E. ...			2 00
"	" with Notes by Heyne, ... E. ...			3 00
"	Æneid, with English Notes, &c. Ed. by Anthon, A. ...			1 25
"	" Ed. by Hunter, ... E. ...			0 88
"	" with English Notes from Dübner. Ed. by Arnold, ... E. ...			1 50
"	" Notes by Anthon. Ed. by Trollope, E. ...			2 00
"	" Do. Ed. by Major, E. ...			1 50
"	Eclogues and Georgics, with Eng. Notes by Anthon, A.			1 25
"	" Notes by Anthon. Ed. by Nicholls, E. ...			1 50
"	" with English Notes from Dübner. Ed. by Arnold, ... E. ...			
"	Bucolics, Oxford Text, with English Notes, E. ...			0 20
"	Georgics. Do. do. do. ... E. ...			0 40
"	" from Forbiger's Text, ... E. ...			0 35

ANTIQUITIES, BIOGRAPHY, MYTHOLOGY, &c.

Adams' Roman Antiquities. Notes by Boyd. ... E. ...		1 50
Ainsworth's Travels in the Track of the Ten Thousand Greeks, E.		2 00
Anthon's Manual of Roman Antiquities, ... A. ...		0 87½
" Do. of Greek Antiquities, ... A. ...		0 87½
" Do. of Greek and Roman Mythology, A. ...		
" Do. of Greek Literature, ... A. ...		1 00
" Do. of Ancient and Mediæval Geography, A. ...		1 50

$ Cts.

Arnold's Hand Book of Grecian Mythology, with outline Engravings, ... E. ... 1 25
" Hand Book of Greek Synonyms, from the French of Pillon, ... E. ... 1 75
" Hand Book of Latin Synonyms, from the German of Doderlain, ... E. ... 1 00
Bojesen's Grecian and Roman Antiquities. Ed. by Arnold, A. ... 1 00
Becker's Gallus, ... E. ... 2 50
" Charicles, ... 2 37½
Browne's Hebrew Antiquities. Ed. by Arnold, ... E. ... 1 00
Dictionary of Classical Quotations, ... E. ... 1 00
Donaldson's Theatre of the Greeks, ... E. ... 4 00
" Varronianus, ... E. ... 3 75
" Cratylus, ... E. ... 5 00
Dwight's Grecian and Roman Mythology, ... A. ... 0 75
Findlay's Classical Atlas. ... ... A. ... 8 25
Greek and Roman Philosophy and Science, by Dr. Newman and others, ... E. ... 1 75
Greek Literature, History of, by Talfourd and others, E. ... 1 00
History of Greece—Chambers' Educational Course, E. ... 0 75
" Greek Literature, by Talfourd and others, E. ... 1 75
" Roman Literature, by Dr. Arnold and others, E. ... 2 75
Hermann's Manual of Grecian Antiquities, ... E. ... 1 00
Hart's Greek and Roman Mythology, ... A. ... 0 50
Hart's New Pantheon, ... E. ... 1 25
Johnston's Classical Atlas, ... E. ... 3 00
King's College Ancient Atlas, ... E. ... 2 00
Liddell's History of Rome, many illustrations, ... A. ... 1 00
Olympus and its inhabitants, by Smith. Ed. by Carmichael, 1 00
Plutarch's Lives, Translated by J. & W. Langhorne, A. ... 1 25
Pillan's Physical and Classical Geography, ... E. ... 1 00
Pillan's First Steps in Classical Geography, ... E. ... 0 50
Pinnock's Catechism of Mythology, ... E. ... 0 20
Putz & Arnold's Ancient Geography and History, A. ... 1 00
Roman Literature, History of, by Dr. Arnold and others, E. ... 3 00
" Antiquities, by Professor Ramsay, maps and illustrations, ... E. ... 2 25
" " by Adams, ... E. ... 1 50
Riley's Dictionary of Classical Quotations, ... E. ... 1 00
Sandford's Rules and Exercises in Homeric and Attic Greek, E. 1 37½
" Introduction to Writing Greek, ... E. ... 0 75
" Extracts from Greek Authors, ... E. ... 1 25
Smith's (Agnes) Olympus and its Inhabitants, ... E. ... 0 88
Smith's Dictionary of Greek and Roman Antiquities, A. ... 4 00
" Smaller do. do. do. E. ... 2 00

			$. Crs.
Smith's Dictionary of Greek and Roman Antiquities,	A.	...	1 00
" Classical Dictionary, ...	A.	...	2 50
" Smaller do.	E.	...	2 00
" Dictionary of Greek and Roman Biography,	A.	...	10 00
Thirwall's History of Greece, ...	A.	...	2 75
Taylor's Manual of Ancient History, ...	A.	...	1 75
Wilkinson's Ancient Egyptians, ...	A.	...	2 00

TRANSLATIONS OF THE CLASSICS.

Æschylus. By an Oxonian. Revised by T. A. Buckley. With an Appendix (not contained in Bohn's volume), embracing all of Hermann's Emendations, translated and explained by Burges, ... **A.** ... 0 75

Cæsar, Commentaries on the Gallic and Civil Wars: with the Supplementary Books attributed to Hirtius; including the Alexandrian, African, and Spanish Wars. Literally Translated, with Notes, and a very copious Index, **A.** ... 0 75

Cicero's Offices; or, Moral Duties: also his Cato Major, an Essay on Old Age; Lælius an Essay on Friendship; Paradoxes; Scipio's Dream; and Letters to Quintus on the Duties of a Magistrate. Literally Translated, with Notes, designed to exhibit a comparative View of the Opinions of Cicero, and those of Modern Moralists and Ethical Philosophers. By Cyrus R. Edmonds, ... **A.** ... 0 75

Cicero's Orations, by Yonge, ... **A.** ... 0 75

Demosthenes. Vol. I. The Olynthiac and other Public Orations of Demosthenes. Vol. II. The Orations of Demosthenes on the Crown, and on the Embassy. Translated with Notes, &c., by Charles Rann Kennedy. 2 vols. ... ... **A.** ... 1 50

Euripides, Literally Translated, with Critical and Explanatory Notes, by T. Alois Buckley, of Christ Church. 2 vols. A. ... 1 50

Herodotus. A New and Literal Version, from the Text of Baehr. With a Geographical and Gen'l Index. By Henry Cary, M.A., Worcester College, Oxford, ... **A.** ... 0 75

Homer's Iliad. Literally Translated, with Explanatory Notes, by Buckley, ... **A.** ... 0 75

Horace. Translated Literally into English Prose, by C. Smart, A. M., of Pembroke College, Cambridge. A new edition, with a copious Selection of Notes, by Theodore Alois Buckley, B.A., of Christ's Church, ... **A.** ... 0 75

Sallust. Florus, and Velleius Paterculus. Literally Translated, with copious Notes and general Index. By the Rev. John Selby Watson, M.A., Head Master of the Proprietary Grammar School, Stockwell, ... **A.** ... 0 75

$ Cts.

Sophocles, in English Prose. The Oxford Translation. New Edition, revised according to the Text of Dindorf, A. ... 0 75

Tacitus. The Oxford Translation, Revised, with Notes. Vol. I. The Annals. Vol. II. The History, Germany, Agricola, and Dialogues on Orators. 2 vols. ... ... A. ... 1 50

Thucydides. A new and Literal Version, from the Text of Arnold, Collated with Bekker, Göller, and Poppo. By the Rev. Henry Dale, M.A, Head Master of the New Proprietary School, Blackheath, and late Demy of Magdalene College, Oxford, ... A. ... 0 75

Virgil. Literally Translated into English Prose, with Notes, by Davidson. A new Edition, Revised, with additional Notes, by Theodore Alois Buckley, of Christ Church, ... A. ... 0 75

Xenophon's Anabasis, or Expedition of Cyrus, and the Memorabilia of Socrates. Literally Translated from the Greek of Xenophon, by the Rev. J. S. Watson, M.A., M.R.S.L. With a Geographical Commentary, by W. F. Ainsworth, Esq., F.S.A., F.R.G.S., F.G.S. ... ... A. ... 0 75

*** We have also a number of the Translations in Bohn's Classical Library (of which the above are reprints). The price is $1 50 per vol.

FRENCH.

Addick's Elements of the French Language,	...	A. ...	0 38
Arnold's Hand Book of French Vocabulary,	...	E. ...	1 25
" First French Book, ...	.,	E. ...	1 50
Badois' Grammar for Frenchmen to learn English,		A. ...	1 00
Bolmar's Levizac's French Grammar, ...	...	A. ...	1 00
" Book of French Verbs, ...	...	A. ...	0 50
Bossuet's French Word and Phrase Book,	...	A. ...	0 37½
Cobbett's French Grammar, ...	...	A. ...	0 75
Collot's Levizac's French Grammar Exercises,	...	A. ...	0 50
" Key to, " " "	...	...	0 37½
" Pronouncing French Reader, ...	...	A. ...	0 50
" Anecdotes and Questions, ...	...	A. ...	0 50
" Dialogues and Phrases, ...	...	A. ...	0 50
" Interlinear French Reader, ...	...	A. ...	0 50
" Dramatic French Reader, ...	...	A. ...	1 00
" French and English Dictionary,	...	A. ...	3 00
De Fiva's Grammaire de Grammaire, ...	...	E. ...	1 00
" Key to " " " ...	...	E. ...	1 00
" Elementary French Reader, ...	...	A. ...	0 50
" Classical do. ...	...	A. ...	1 00
De Porquet's New Parisian Grammar, ...	...	E. ...	1 00
" Key to, ...	...	...	0 30
" French Spelling Book, ...	...	E. ...	0 75

			$ Crs.
De Porquet's Parisian Phraseology,	... ...	E. ...	0 75
" " Ed. by Sales,	...	A. ...	0 90
" Trésor de l'Ecolier Francais,	...	E. ...	1 00
" Sequel to do., E., $1. Key to do.,	...	E. ...	1 00
" Traducteur Francais,	... ...	E. ...	1 00
" First French Reading Book,	...	A. ...	0 75
De Perac's French as spoken in Paris,	... ...	A. ...	0 75
Green's Primary Lessons in French,	...	Montreal,	0 30
" do. do.	... ...	A. ...	0 50
" Companion to Ollendorff's French method,		A. ...	0 75
Grandineau's Le Petit Precepteur,	... ...	E. ...	0 90
" Conversations Familieres.			
Haas' Introduction to the French Language,	...	E. ...	0 45
Hamel's French Grammar,	... ...	E. ...	1 10
James and Moles' Dictionary,	... ...	A. ...	2 50
Levizac's French Grammar,	... ...	Quebec,	0 75
" do. Edited by Bolmar,	...	A. ...	1 00
" do. " Collot,	...		0 50
Letellier's Grammaire Francaise,	, ...	Paris, ...	0 62½
" Participes, ...	... ...	Paris, ...	0 50
" Conjugaison,	... ...	Paris, ...	0 50
L'Abeille pour les Enfans,	... ...	Montreal,	0 25
" New, ...	... ...	Paris, ...	0 50
Merlet's French Grammar,	... ...	E. ...	1 50
" La Traducteur,	... ...	E. ...	1 50
" Dictionary of Difficulties,	... ...	E. ...	1 75
Moul's French Companion,	... ...	A. ...	0 30
Noel & Chapsal's Grammaire Francaise, ...	...	A. ...	0 75
" do. with Exercises,	A. ...		1 00
Ollendorff's New Method of learning French, by Jewett,	A. ...		1 00
" Key to do. ...	...		0 75
" " by Value, $1. Key to do.	...		0 75
Ostervald's Novum Testamentum,	... ...	A. ...	0 37½
Perrin's French Conversations, ...	... ...	A. ...	0 25
" " Spelling,	... ...	E. ...	0 55
" Fables, Ed. by Bolmar, with Key,	...	A. ...	0 75
Porny's French Spelling,	... ...	E. ...	0 65
Picot Charles, No. 1. First Lessons in French,	...	A. ...	0 60
" No. 2. French Student's Assistant,		A. ...	0 30
" No. 3. Historical Narration in French,		A. ...	0 75
" No. 4. Scientific do.		A. ...	0 90
Roemer's Study of French (Mezzofanti's System),		A. ...	1 00
" First French Reader, ...	... ...	A. ...	1 00
" Second do. ...	... ...	A. ...	1 25
Roy Histoire du Canada,	... ...	Montreal,	0 50

				$ Crs.
Spiers and Surenne's French Dictionary ...	...	A. ...	1 50	
" " unabridged,	...	A. ...	3 00	
Surenne's French Pronouncing Dictionary,	...	E. ...	3 00	
" do.	...	A. ...	0 90	
" New French Manual, ...	...	A. ...	0 62½	
" Pronouncing French Primer, ...	...	E. ...	0 45	
Wanostrocht's French Grammar,	...	A. ...	0 75	
Wilson's Guide to French Grammar,	...	A. ...	0 50	

FRENCH CLASSICS, &c.

Abaillard et Heloise ...	... Paris, ...	0 88
Balzac (H. de) Theatre,	... Paris, ...	0 88
Boileau, Poésies complètes,	... Paris, ...	0 75
Buffon. Histoire des Animaux, ...	... Paris, ...	0 88
Burns, R., Poésies, traduites par De Wailly,	... Paris, ...	0 75
Bossuet, Sermons,	... Paris, ...	0 75
Cervantes, Histoire de Don Quichotte de la Manche, Paris, ...		0 50
Cottin, (Mme.) Elizabeth,	A. ...	0 50
Corneille, Œuvres, ...	... Paris, ...	0 90
Chateaubriand, Atala, Réné Voyage en Amerique, &c. Paris, ...		0 88
" Genie du Christianisme, 2 vols.,	... Paris, ...	1 50
" Les Martyrs,	... Paris, ...	0 75
" Les Natchez,	... Paris, ...	0 75
" Etudes Historiques,	... Paris, ...	0 75
Dante, La Divine Comédie,	... Paris, ...	0 88
De Foe, Adventures de Robinson Crusoe, ...	... Paris, ...	0 75
Diderot, Œuvres Choises, 2 vols....	... Paris, ...	1 50
Elizabeth, Mme. Cottin,	A. ...	0 50
Fleury, Histoire de France,	E. ...	0 80
Florian, Fables,	... Paris, ...	0 30
Fenelon, Adventures de Télémaque, Ed. par Bolmar,	A. ...	0 55
" " Ed. par Surenne,	A. ...	0 50
" " Ed. par Lebrun,	A. ...	0 75
Girardin, (Mme.) Lettrès Parisiennes,	... Paris, ...	0 38
Goethe, LeFaust,	... Paris, ...	0 88
Guizot, Washington et Histoire des Etats-Unis,	... Paris, ...	1 00
" (Mme.) Récréationes Morales, Contes,	... Paris, ...	1 00
Gil Blas, Extracts from...	... Quebec,	0 38
Histoire de France, par Mme. Saint Ouèn,	... Paris, ...	0 40
Héloise et Abaillard, ...	... Paris, ...	0 88
La Petit Robinson,	... A. ...	0 50
La Fontaine, Fables, ...	... A. ...	0 60
LeSage, Histoire de Gil Blas,	... Quebec,	0 38
La Rochefocauld, Maximes,	... Paris, ...	0 75
Massillon, Petit, Carême et Sermons,	... Paris, ...	0 75

			$ Cts.
Marmontel, Elements de Littérature, ...	... Paris, ...	2 50
Mennechet, Histoire de France, ...	... Paris, ...	1 75
Milton, Le Paradise perdu, ...	... Paris, ...	0 88
Moliere Œuvres, 2 vols., ...	... Paris, ...	1 50
Nicole, Œuvres, Philosophiques et Morales,	... Paris, ...	0 88
Oraisons Funebres de Bossuet, &c. &c., 2 vols.	... Paris, ...	1 75
Pascal, Les Pensées, arie les Pensees de Nicole,	.... Paris, ...	0 75
" Les Provinciales, ...	... Paris, ...	0 75
Paul et Virginie, ...	... A. ...	0 50
Poésies, Selections for Young Persons, ...	... A. ...	1 25
Racine, Œuvres, complete, ...	... Paris, ...	0 75
Rémusat, (Mme. de) Essai sur l'Education des femmes, Paris, ...	0 88
Robertson, Histoire de Charles, Quint, ...	... Paris, ...	1 75
Rousseau Les Confessions, ...	... Paris, ...	0 75
" La Nouvelle Héloise, ...	.. Paris, ...	0 75
Saint Ouen, Histoire de France, ...	... Paris, ...	0 40
Schiller, Théâtre, 2 vols., ...	... Paris, C..	1 75
Swift, Voyages de Gullivre.	... Paris, ...	0 88
St. Pierre, Paul et Virginie, ...	... A. ...	0 50
Thierry Lettres sur l'Histoire de France, ...	... Paris, ...	1 00
Telemaque, par Fenelon, ...	... A. ...	0 50
Voltaire, Classiques, ...	... Paris, ...	0 25
" Henriade, ...	... Paris, ...	0 90
" Siecle de Louis XIV., ...	... Paris, ...	0 75
" La Henriade, ...	... Paris, ...	0 75
" Contes, Satires, Epitres, ...	... Paris, ...	0 75
" Theatre, ...	... Paris, ...	0 75
" Histoire de Charles XII., ...	... Paris, ...	0 75
Washington, Vie de Washington, ...	... Paris, ...	2 50
Zimmerman, De la Solitude, ...	... Paris, ...	0 88

GERMAN.

Adler's Progressive German Reader, ...	... A. ...	1 00
" German Dictionary, ...	... A. ...	3 50
" " " abridged, ...	... A. ...	1 50
" Hand-book of German Literature,	... A. ...	1 50
Ahn's Method of Learning German, ...	... A. ...	0 40
Eichorn's Practical German Grammar, ...	... A. ...	1 00
Gerlach's German and English Dictionary, ...	E. ...	1 50
Heydenreich's Elementary German Reader,	... A. ...	
Ollendorf's New Method of Learning German, edited by Adler, ...	... A. ...	1 00
Oswald's German Reader, ...	... B. ..	0 75
" " " abridged, ...	... E. ...	0 38
Œhlschlager's Pronouncing German Reader, ...	A. ...	1 00

B

		$ Cr s
Roemer's Polyglot Reader, ...	A. ...	1 00
Sternes' German Reader, ...	A. ...	1 70

ITALIAN, SPANISH, HEBREW AND GREEK TEXT BOOKS.

ENGLISH SCHOOL BOOKS.

TEXT BOOKS FOR COMMON SCHOOLS—Published under the direction of the Commissioners of National Education in Ireland—prepared by practical and experienced Masters—and recommended by the Council of Public Instruction for Upper Canada, to be used in Canadian Schools.

	4 cts. each,	25 cts. ℔ doz.	
First Book of Lessons, ...	13	" 1 00	"
Second " "	13	" 1 10	"
Sequel to Second Book, ...	20	" 2 00	"
Third Book of Lessons, ...	25	" 2 50	"
Fourth " "	34	" 3 25	"
Fifth " " (Boys')	30	" 3 00	"
Sixth, or Reading Books for Girls' School,	25	" 2 25	"
Introduction to the Art of Reading, ...	20	" 1 75	"
Spelling Book Superseded, by Prof. Sullivan	17	" 1 50	"
Canada Spelling Book, ...	13	" 1 00	"
Mavor's " "	13	" 1 00	"
Cobb's " "	13	" 1 00	"
Carpenter's " "	13	" 1 00	"
English Grammar, ...	37½	" 4 00	"
Epitome of Geographical Knowledge, ...	13	" 1 25	"
Compendium of " " ...			
Introduction to Geography and History, by			
Sullivan, ...	25	" 2 50	"
First Arithmetic, ...	13	" 1 00	"
Key to "	13	" 1 25	"
Arithmetic, in Theory and Practice, ...	50	" 4 50	"
Key to " " ...	75	" 0 00	"
Thompson's Arithmetic, ...	75	" 8 00	"
Book-keeping, ...	20	" 2 00	"
Key to "	20	" 2 00	"
Elements of Geometry, ...	15	" 1 50	"
Mensuration, ...	30	" 3 00	"
Appendix to do.	20	" 2 00	"
Lessons on the Truth of Christianity, ...	13	" 1 25	"
Lennie's English Grammar, ...	17	" 1 50	"
Key to " "	75	" 7 50	"
Morse's Geography, ...	50	" 5 25	"
Kirkham's English Grammar, ...	40	" 4 00	"
Set Tablet Lessons, Spelling and Reading.	25	"	

ARITHMETIC.

Arithmetic in Theory and Practice,	...	... Toronto,	0 50
Key to " " "	...	... "	0 75
Bonnycastle's Arithmetic, Edited by Tyson,	...	... E. ..	0 88
Key to " "	...	... E. ...	1 00
Brass' Mental Arithmetic,	...	... Toronto,	0 50
Colenso's Elementary Arithmetic,	...	... E. ...	0 63
Davis' Arithmetic, ...	...	... A. ...	0 38
Docharty's Commercial Arithmetic,	...	... A. ...	0 75
Dodd's Elementary Arithmetic,...	...	... A. ...	0 38
" High School, "	...	... A. ...	0 75
" Key to the above,	...	... A. ...	0 38
Gouinlock's Arithmetic,	...	... Toronto,	0 45
Hutton's Arithmetic,	...	... E. ...	1 75
Ingram's Arithmetic,	...	... Toronto,	0 50
" Key to " ...	...	... " ...	0 75
Loomis' Arithmetic, Theoretical and Practical,	...	A. ...	0 75
Melrose's Arithmetic, ...	...	... E. ...	0 40
Murray's " ...	...	... E. ...	0 50
National First Book of Arithmetic,	...	... Toronto,	0 12½
" " " Key,		... Toronto,	0 17
" Second "	...	... Toronto,	0 37½
" " " Key,		... Toronto,	0 75
Stoddart's Juvenile Mental Arithmetic, ...		... A. ...	0 12½
" Intellectual Arithmetic,	...	... A. ...	0 20
" Practical "	...	... E. ...	0 40
Smith's (Barnard) Arithmetic, ...	...	... E. ...	1 25
Thomson's Arithmetic,	...	... E. ...	0 75
" Key to "	...	... E. ...	1 50
Walkinghame's Tutors' Assistant,	...	... Toronto,	0 25
" Key to "	...	... " ...	1 20

ASTRONOMY.

Burritt's Geography of the Heavens; a Class Book of Astronomy, with Celestial Atlas,	...	A. ...	1 25
Christian Knowledge Society's Astronomical Figures 12 Plates,	... ...	... E. ...	1 50
Dick's Solar System, ...	...	... A. ...	0 70
" Celestial Scenery,	...	... A. ...	0 45
" Sidereal Heavens,	...	... A. ...	0 45
" Practical Astronomer, ...	...	... A. ...	0 45
Herschell's Treatise on Astronomy, with Questions.		A. ...	0 75
Hind's Astronomical Vocabulary,	...	... E. ...	0 37½
Johnston's School Atlas of Astronomy, ...		... E. ...	3 00
Keith on the Use of the Globes,	...	... E. ...	1 25

						$ Cts.
Key to Keith on the Use of the Globes	...	...	E.	...	0 75
Mattison's Astronomical Maps, or Celestial Charts, designed to illustrate the Mechanism of the Heavens,	...	...	E.	...	18 00
Mattison's Elementary Astronomy, to accompany the foregoing Maps,	...	...	E.	...	0 60
		...	E.	...	1 50
Nichol's Planetary System,	...	...	A.	...	0 75
Olmsted's Astronomy,	...	...	E.	...	0 20
Pinnock's Catechism of the Globes,	...	...	E.	...	0 20
" " of Astronomy,	...	...	A.	...	1 00
Reid's Astronomy,	...	...	E.	...	0 25
Reynolds' Atlas of Astronomy, 10 Plates, with description,	...	...	E.	...	0 50

" " the above with the Plates coloured

" Astronomical Diagrams; a set of Twelve, exhibiting the principal Astronomical Phenomena. The following are transparancies: 1. Chart of the Heavens; 2. The Solar System; 3. View of the Moon; 4. The Sun and Solar Phenomena; 5, Comparative Magnitude of the Planets, in portfolio, ... E. ... 3 00

Smith's Illustrated Astronomy, ... A. ... 0 80

Whewell's Astronomy and General Physics, ... A. ... 0 50

ASTRONOMICAL APPARATUS.

The following apparatus are of Canadian manufacture, that portion of the work which comes within our department having been executed by ourselves. We can confidently say that these apparatus are equal to any imported, and at much lower prices:—

The TELLURIAN is designed to illustrate the various phenomena resulting from the relations of the Sun, Moon and Earth to each other; the succession of day and night, the change of the seasons, the change of the Sun's declination, the different lengths of day and night, the changes of the moon, the harvest moon, the precession of the equinoxes, the differences of a solar and sidereal year, &c. The Moon revolves around the Earth, and both together around the Sun, while Sun, Earth and Moon revolve around a common centre of gravity. Price, $6.00.

The PLANETARIUM or ORRERY, represents the proportional size and relative position of the Planets composing the Solar System, except the asteroids, and shows their annual revolutions. A correct idea of the Solar System is seldom received, except by such aid. With it we see the Planets and their Moons circling round their common centre, each in its separate orbit, and occupying its own place in the Ecliptic—and system is devolved from the seeming chaos of the stars. Price, $10.

$ Crs.

BOOK-KEEPING.

Duff's American Accountant ...	...	...	A.	... 0 75
Fulton & Eastman's Book-keeping	...	...	A.	... 0 62½
Hutton's Practical "	...	...	E.	... 0 50
Inglis's "	(Chamber's E. C.)	E.	... 0 60
" "	Single Entry ...	E.	... 0 35
Jackson's Practical "	...	...	A.	... 1 00
Marsh's Book-keeping by Single Entry (printed in colors) A.	... 0 75
" " by Double Entry " " A.	... 1 25
National Series Book-keeping ...	...	... Toronto.	0 20
Key to do.	...	... Toronto.	0 17
Palmer's Elementary Book-keeping	...	... A.	... 0 20

BOTANY.

Chamber's Vegetable Physiology	...	...	E.	... 0 45
Gray's Botanical Text Book ...	...	...	A.	... 1 75
Green's Primary Class Book of Botany ...	...	A.	... 0 75
" Analytical Class Book of Botany	...	A.	... 1 50
Hooker's Child's Book of Nature—Plants	...	A.	... 0 50
Paxton's Botanical Dictionary ...	...	...	E.	... 0 00
Pinnock's Catechism of Botany	...	...	E.	... 0 20
Reynolds's Range of Vegetation, and the Snow Line (colored Diagram, showing the arrangement of vegetation in all latitudes) ... ... E. ... 0 37½
Wood's First Book of Botany ...	...	...	A.	... 0 50
" Class " " ...	...	...	A.	... 1 25

CHEMISTRY.

Comstock's Elements of Chemistry	...	...	A.	... 0 75
Forster's Chemistry ...	...	...	A.	... 0 60
Fowne's Elementary Chemistry	...	...	E.	... 0 30
Gardner's Chemistry ...	...	...	A.	... 0 25
Hooker's Child's Book of Nature—Air, Water, Heat and Light ... ... A. ... 0 50
Johnston's Agricultural Chemistry, Ed. by Brown	A.	... 1 00
" Catechism of do. ...	...	...	E.	... 0 25
Johnson's Chemistry of Common Life, 2 vols.	...	A.	... 2 00
Morfitt's Chemical Manipulation	...	...	A.	... 4 00
" Applied Chemistry ...	...	...	A.	... 5 00
Pinnock's Catechism of Chemistry	...	...	E.	... 0 20
Reid's Rudiments of Chemistry (Chambers, E. C.)	E.	... 0 75
Reid & Bain's Chemistry ...	...	...	A.	... 1 00
Stockhart's Principles of Chemistry	...	...	A.	... 1 12½

			$ Cts.
Youman's Class Book of Chemistry	...	A. ...	0 75
" Chemical Atlas (13 colored plates)	...	E. ...	2 00

COMPOSITION.

Parker's Exercises in Composition	...	A. ...	0 37½
Quackenbos's First Lessons in Composition	...	A. ...	0 50
" Advanced Course of do. and Rhetoric		A. ...	1 00
		E. ...	0 50
Reid's Rudiments of English Composition	...	E. A.	0 88
" " Key to	... ...	E. ...	0 60
" English Composition	.. ...	...	A. ...	1 00
Wilson on Punctuation	... ...		

ELOCUTION, &c.

Ewing's Principles of Elocution	...	E. ...	1 00
Fitz's School Exhibition	... ...	A. ...	0 37½
How's Practical Elocutionist	... ...	A. ...	1 00
Knowles' Rhetorical Reader	... ...	A. ...	0 62½
McCulloch's Extracts, in prose and verse	...	E. ...	0 55
Rede's Speaker	... ...	E. ...	0 75
Souter's Reader	... ...	E. ...	0 85
Scott's Lessons in Elocution	... ...	E. ...	0 55

ENGLISH DICTIONARIES.

Crabbe's English Synonymes	...	A. ...	2 00
Graham's English Synonymes, Ed by		A. ...	1 00
Johnson's Pocket Dictionary	... ...	E. ...	0 25
" " "	... ...	E. ...	0 38
Reid's English Dictionary	... ...	A. ...	0 90
Sullivan's " "	... ...	E. ...	0 88
Walker's Pronouncing Dictionary, with Key	...	E. ...	1 12½
" School "	...	Montreal.	0 38
Webster's American Dictionary, unabridged, 4to ...		A. ...	6 00
" " " 8vo (the whole of the words in the 4to edition are also in this, but the definitions are abridged)		A. ...	3 50
Whateley's English Synonymes	... ...	A. ...	0 50

ENGLISH LANGUAGE.

Crabb's English Synonymes	... ...	E. ...	2 00
Craik Outlines of History of the English Language		E. ...	1 00
Fowler's English Language	... ...	A. ...	1 50
" " abridged ...		A. ...	1 00
Graham's English Synonymes, Ed. by Reed		A. ...	1 00
Harrison's English Language	... ...	A. ...	1 00
Latham's Hand Book of the English Language ...		A. ...	1 00

$ Crs.

Prefixes and Affixes of the English Language, sheets, Toronto.			0 50
Roget's English Thesaurus	...	A.	1 50
Sullivan's Dictionary of Derivations	...	E.	0 62½
Trench's English, Past and Present	...	A.	0 75
Trench on the Study of Words	...	A.	0 75
Whateley's English Synonymes	...	A.	0 62½
Wilson's English Punctuation	...	A.	0 88

ENGLISH AND FOREIGN LITERATURE.

American Literature, Chambers' Hand Book of	...	E.	1 00
Brandes' Cyclopædia of Literature, Science and Art		A.	4 00
British Poets (Selections from), 2 vols	...	E.	0 75
" Biographical Sketches of, national series,		E.	0 50
Chambers' History of the English Language and Liter.		E.	0 75
" Cyclopædia of English Literature	...	E.	4 00
Cleveland's Compendium of " "	...	A.	1 50
" English Literature of the XIXth Century,		A.	1 50
Craik's Literature and Science in England, 3 vols		E.	1 75
Foster's European Literature	...	A.	1 00
French Literature, Chambers' Hand Book of	...	E.	1 00
German " " "	...	E.	0 75
Italian " " "	...	E.	1 00
Sandford's Rise and Progress of Literature	...	E.	0 62½
Sismondi's Literature of Europe (Bohn's Lib.) 2 vols.		E.	2 00
Spalding's English Literature	...	A.	1 00
Spanish Literature, Chambers' Hand Book of	...	E.	1 00

GEOGRAPHY.

Anthon's Ancient and Mediæval Geography	...	A.	1 50
" " " "	...	A.	1 75
Beavan's Ancient Geography	...	E.	0 75
Butler's Geographica Classica	...	A.	0 75
Cornell's First Steps in Geography	...	A.	0 25
" Primary "	...	A.	0 50
" Intermediate "	...	A.	0 67
" High School Geography and Atlas	...	A.	1 75
Colton and Fitch's Modern Geography, ...	...	A.	0 75
Compendium of Geography, National Series,	...	A.	
Epitome of Geography, National Series, ...	...	A.	0 50
Ewing's Canadian School Geography, ...	...	Toronto,	0 15
Fitch's Physical Geography, ...	...	A.	1 00
Gaskin's Geography, ...	...	E.	0 45
Goldsmith's Grammer of Geography, by Wright, ...		E.	1 00
Gouinlock's Geography	...	Toronto,	0 50
Groombridge's Catechism of Geography, ...	...	E.	0 10

		$ Cts.
Groombridge's Catechism of Physical Geography,	E. ...	0 20
Hodgins' Easy Lessons in British Geography, sheets, Toronto,		0 50
" Geography and History of British North America, ...Toronto,		0 50
Keith on the Globes	E. ...	1 12½
Koeppen's World in the Middle Ages, 2 vols. and Atlas,...	A. ...	4 50
Lippincott's Pronouncing Gazeteer of the World ...	A. ...	6 00
Maury's Physical Geography of the Sea, ...	A. ...	1 50
Mitchell's Geography and Atlas, ...	A. ...	1 25
Morse's School Geography, ...	A. ...	0 50
Olney's Modern Geography and Atlas, ...	A. ...	1 00
Parker's Geographical Questions, ...	A. ...	0 20
Physical Geography, Catechism of, ...	E. ...	0 20
Putz and Arnold's Ancient Geography and History,	A. ...	1 00
" " Mediæval, " "	A. ...	0 75
" " Modern, " "	A. ...	1 00
Pillan's Physical and Classical Geography ...	E. ...	1 00
" First Steps, " " ...	E. ...	0 50
Pinnock's Catechism of Geography, ...Toronto,		0 12½
" " of British Geography, ...	E. ...	0 20
" " of Ancient, ...	E. ...	0 20
Reid, (Alex.) Rudiments of Geography, ...	E. ...	0 25
" Outlines of Sacred Geography, ...S	E. ...	0 12½
" (Hugo) System of Modern Geography	E. ...	0 60
Reynold's Geographical Diagrams and 12 Plates, in portfolio, ...	E. ...	3 00
Smith's Geography, ...	A. ...	0 75
Somerville's Physical Geography	A. ...	1 25
Stewart's Modern Geography, ...	E. ...	1 00
Sullivan's Introduction to Geography, ...	E. ...	0 20
" Geography Generalised, ...	E. ...	0 50
White's Geography, ...	E. ...	0 30

ATLASES.

Ancient Geography, Atlas of, ...	E. ...	2 00
Canadian School Atlas ... ...Montreal,		0 50
Chambers' "	E. ...	3 00
" Primer Atlas, 9 Maps, ...	E. ...	0 75
Dowers' School Atlas of Modern Geography ...	E. ...	3 00
" Minor, " " " ...	E.	
" Short, " " " ...	B. ...	1 00
Groombridge's Shilling Atlas	E. ...	0 25
Harrow Modern Atlas, ...	E. ...	3 50
Harrow Modern Atlas, Junior, ...	E. ...	2 00

				$ Crs.
Harrow Classical Atlas,	... ...	E.	...	3 50
" " Junior,	... ...	E.	...	2 00
Johnston's Elementary School Atlas,	... ...	E.	...	1 75
" General,	... ...	E.	...	3 00
" Physical, ...	... ...	E.	...	3 00
" Classical, ...	... ...	E.	...	3 00
" Physical Atlas of Natural Phenomena,		E.	...	12 50
Morse's North American Atlas,	... . .	A.	...	3 00
Peterman's Atlas of Physical Geography,	...	E.	...	5 00
" " Political " ...	...	E.	...	7 50
Stanford's Complete Atlas,	... ...	E.	...	54 00
" Library, " ...	... ...	E.	...	42 00
" Family, ...	... ...	E.	...	18 00
" Cyclopedian,	... ...	E.	...	6 00

GEOLOGY AND MINERALOGY.

Comstock's Elements of Geology,	... ...	A.	...	1 00
Dana's Manual of Mineralogy, ...	... ...	A.	...	1 25
Hitchcock's Elementary Geology,	... ...	A.	...	1 25
Loomis' Elements of Geology, ...	... ...	A.	...	0 75
Lyell's Manual of Elementary Geology, ...	...	A.	...	2 25
" Principles of Geology, ...	... ...	A.	...	2 25
Page's Elements of Geology, ...	... ...	A.	...	0 75
Pinnock's Catechism of Geology,	... ...	E.	...	0 20
Rudiments of Mineralogy, (Weales' series,)	...	E.	...	0 30
Reynolds' Atlas of Geology,	... ...	E.	...	0 25
" " Coloured,	... ...	E.	...	0 50
" Geognostic Profiles, showing the relief of Continents, &c.,	... ...	E.	...	1 50
" Geological Diagrams, 12 in the series, in portfolio,	... ...	E.	...	3 00

GRAMMAR.—(See also English Language.)

Allen and Cornwell's English Grammar, ...	...	E.	...	0 55
Arnold's English Grammar, ...	... ...	E.	...	1 00
Bullion's Practical Lessons in English Grammar,		A.	...	0 20
" Analytical and Practical Grammar,		A.	...	0 62½
Chamber's Introduction to Grammar,	... ...	E.	...	0 35
" Grammar and Composition,	... ...	E.	...	0 60
Fowler's English Grammar,	... ...	A.	...	1 00
Kirkham's English Grammar	... ...	Toronto,		0 50
Lennie's English Grammar,	... ...	Toronto,		0 15
" Key to "	... ...	E.	...	0 90
Murray's English Grammar, ...	... ...	Montreal,		0 25
MacCulloch's English Grammar,	... ...	E.	...	0 40

		$ Cts.
National School Grammar, ...	... Toronto,	0 12½
Pinnock's Catechism of English Grammar,	... E. ...	0 20
Stoddart's Universal Grammar,... ...	... E. ...	1 50
Town's Analysis of the English Language,	... A. ...	0 25

HISTORY.

Ancient History, Chamber's Educational course, ...	E. ...	0 75
" " Pinnock's Catechism of ...	E. ...	0 20
" " Taylor's Manual of ...	A. ..	1 25
" " and Geography, by Putz and Arnold,	A. ...	1 00
" and Modern History, Hinck's Summary of,	E. ...	0 88
Bible and Gospel History, Pinnock's Catechism of,	Toronto,	0 12½
" " " ...	... E. ...	0 20
" " Wilson's, "	... E. ...	0 20
Blair's Chronological Tables, ...	... E. ...	2 75
British Empire, Chamber's History of, ...	... E. ...	0 62½
" " Catechism of,	... Toronto,	0 12½
Bonnechose's History of France, ...	... E. ...	1 25
Child's History of England, (Dickens,) 2 vols.,	... A. ...	0 75
" Greece, (Bonner,) "	... A. ...	1 00
" Rome, " "	... A. ...	1 00
" United States " "	... A. ...	1 00
Canada, Hodgins' History and Geography of,	... Toronto,	0 50
" Roy's History of, ...	... Montreal,	0 50
Chronology, Pinnock's Catechism of, ...	... E. ...	0 20
Chronological Tables, (Blair's,)... ...	... E. ...	2 75
Edwards' Summary of English History ...	... E. ...	0 12½
England, Chamber's History of, ...	... E. ...	0 25
" Dickens, Child's, " 2 vols. ...	... A. ...	0 75
" Marget's, " " ...	... E. ...	1 50
" Markham's, (by Robbins), ...	... A. ...	0 75
" Milner's History of	... E. ...	1 25
" Parker's, "	... E. ...	0 37½
" Pinnock's, "	... A. ...	0 75
" " Whittaker's	... E. ...	1 50
" Simpson's Goldsmith's, " ...	... E. ...	1 00
" White's, " ...	... E. ...	0 37½
" Pinnock's Catechism of, ...	... Montreal,	0 12½
" Wilson's, " ...	... E. ...	0 20
Europe, Alison's History of, abridged for Schools	A. ...	1 25
France, Markham's History of ...	... A. ...	1 00
" Pinnock's " " ...	... A. ...	0 75
" " Catechism do., ...	... E. ...	0 20
" White's History of	... E. ...	0 88
Gibbon, The Student's, by Dr. Smith, ...	... A. ...	1 00

		$ Crs.
General History, Tytler's Elements of	E.	1 10
Greece, Chamber's History of	E.	0 75
" Child's History of (Bonner) 2 vols.,	A.	1 00
" Keightley's History of	A.	1 00
" Lieven's Outlines of the History of (Weale's series)	E.	0 75
" Parker's History of	E.	0 25
" Pinnock's Goldsmith's History of	A.	0 75
" " Catechism of " "	E.	0 20
" Sewell's History of	A.	0 62½
" Simpson's Goldsmith's History of	E.	1 00
" Smith's (Ed. by Greene,) History of	A.	1 00
" Towns' Analysis of " "	E.	0 60
" Whittaker's Pinnock's " "	E.	1 50
Great Britain and Ireland, White's " "	E.	0 75
Harper's School History, A. cloth $1, sheep		1 25
Ireland, Pinnock's Catechism of History of	E.	0 20
Mangnall's Historical Questions, Ed. by Lawrance,	A.	1 00
" " Ed. by Wright & Guy,	E.	1 25
" " Ed. by Birkin	E.	1 25
Mediæval History, Chambers' Ed. course,	E.	0 75
" by Putz,	A.	0 75
Middle Ages, Koeppen's History of, 2 vols., with Atlas,	A.	4 50
Modern History, and Ancient, Hincks' Summary of	E.	0 88
" and Geography, by Putz,	A.	1 00
" Taylor's Manual of	A.	1 50
" Wilson's Catechism of	E.	0 20
Outlines of History, Parker,	A.	1 00
Rome, Chambers' History of	E.	0 62½
" Childs' " by Bonner, 2 vols.,	A.	1 00
" Leivens' Outlines of History of (Weales' series,)	E.	0 75
" Gibbon, (The Student's)	A.	1 00
" Liddell's School History of	A.	1 00
" Parker's History of	E.	0 25
" Pinnock's Goldsmith's History of	A.	0 75
" " Catechism of "	E.	0 20
" Whittaker's History of	E.	1 50
" Simpson's History of	E.	0 75
" Town's Analysis of History of	A.	0 60
Sacred History, White's	E.	0 37½
Scripture History, Pinnock's Catechism of	E.	0 20
" " Watt's	E.	0 45
Scotland, Pinnock's Catechism of History of	E.	0 20
" Simpson's History of	E.	1 00
" White's "	E.	0 45

$ Crs

Taylor's Manual of History			
Turner's Analysis of English and French History	E.	...	0 60
United States, Child's History of (Bonner) 2 vols....	A.	...	1 00
" Quackenbos' History of ...	... A.	...	1 00
Universal History, Parker's	... A.	...	1 00
" White's Elements of ...	... E.		
" " Outlines of ...	... E.	...	0 50
" Worcester's ...	... A.	...	1 00

LITERATURE.—(See English and Foreign Literature.)

LOGIC.

Gerhart's Philosophy and Logic, ...	A.	...	1 00
Lessons on Reasoning	E.	...	0 50
Mills' Logic, ...	A.	...	1 50
Tappen's Elements of Logic, ...	A.	...	1 25
Whateley's Logic, ...	E.	...	0 75
" "	A.	...	0 37½
" Lessons on Reasoning	A.	...	0 60
Wilson's Elementary Treatise on Logic,	A.	...	1 25

MATHEMATICS.

Algebra, Allsop's	A.	...	1 00
" Bridge's Elements of ...	A.	...	0 62½
" Bonnycastle's	A.	...	0 62½
" Clarke's Elements of	A.	...	1 00
" Colenso's. Part I., ...	E.	...	1 12½
" " " Key, ...	E.	...	1 25
" " " II. ...	E.	...	1 50
" " " " ...	E.	...	1 25
" " Elements of. Complete in 1 vol.	E.	...	3 50
" " Miscellaneous Examples and Equation Papers, from Parts I. and II., ...	E.	...	0 75
" Davies' Elementary	A.	...	0 75
" Docharty's Institutes of ...	A.	...	0 75
" Hackley's "	A.	...	1 00
" Loomis's Elements of	A.	...	0 62½
" " Treatise on	A.	...	1 00
" McGauley's, in Theory and Practice ...	E.	...	0 50
" Perkins' Elements of	A.	...	0 75
" " Treatise on	A.	...	1 50
" Sangster's Formulæ	Toronto.		0 12½
" Wood's. Edited by Lund, ...	E.	...	3 00
Calculus, Church's Differential and Integral ...	A.	...	1 50
" Coxe's Treatise on the Integral. (Weale's series.)	E.	...	0 30

		$ Cts.
Calculus, Davies' Differential and Integral ...	A. ...	1 50
" Harris' Examples on the Integral. (Weale's series.)	E. ...	0 30
" Haddon's Examples on the Differential. (Weale's series.)	E. ...	0 30
" Thompson's Differential and Integral, ...	E. ...	1 62½
Dynamics and Statics. Cherriman's, ...	Toronto,	1 00
" (Weale's series.) ...	E. ...	0 45
Euclid, Chambers' Elements of	E. ...	0 75
" Colenso's " ...	E. ...	1 12½
" " with Key to Problems, ...	E. ...	1 62½
" Playfair's Elements of	A. ...	1 00
" Pott's "	E. ...	1 00
" Rutherford's Simson's	E. ...	1 00
" Williams Symbolical	E. ...	1 75
Geometry, Chambers' Plane	E. ...	0 75
" " Solid	E. ...	0 75
" Colenso's Problems and Key, ...	E. ...	1 00
" Davies Legendre, ...	A. ...	1 00
" Hackley's Elementary	A. ...	0 75
" Heather's Descriptive. (Weale's series.)	E, ...	0 60
" Hutton's, by Rutherford, ...	E. ...	1 00
" Loomis's Elements of and Conic Sections,	A. ...	0 75
" National School	Toronto,	0 15
" Perkins' Elements of	A. ...	1 00
" " Plane and Solid ...	A. ...	1 50
" Pinnock's Catechism of	E. ...	0 20
" Wallace's	E. ...	1 50
Hydrostatics. Chambers' Ed. course, ...	E. ...	0 25
Mathematics, Chambers'. Part I., $1 ; Part II.,...	E. ...	1 20
" Comtes Philosophy of	A. ...	1 25
" Ingram's System of	E. ...	2 00
" Davies Practical	A. ...	0 90
" Hutton's Course of ,... ...	E. ...	3 00
" " Key to do., by Hickie, ...	E. ...	1 75
" " Recreations in	E. ...	3 00
Mathematical Dictionary and Cyclopædia of Mathematical Science, ...	A. ...	3 00
Mechanics. Practical, Cherriman's	Toronto,	1 00
" Pinnock's Catechism of	E. ...	0 20
" and Mechanism, Burn's	E. ...	0 50
" and Hydraulics, Ewbanks	A. ...	
" Snowball's	E. ...	2 50
Mensuration, Bonnycastle's	A. ...	0 75
" " Key to do., ...	A. ...	0 75

		$ CTS.
Mensuration, National System, ...	Toronto,	0 25
" " " Appendix to do. ...	" ...	0 15
Optics, Pinnock's Catechism of ...	E. ...	0 20
" Chambers'	E. ...	0 30
Statics, ... (Weale's series.)	E. ...	0 45
" and Dynamics, by Cherriman, ...	Toronto,	1 00
Surveying, Gummere's Treatise on ...	A. ...	1 50
" " Key to do. ...	A. ...	1 12½
" Gillespie's Treatise on ...	A. ...	2 00
Trigonometry, Hutton's. Ed. by Rutherford, ...	E. ...	1 75
" Hackley's		
" Snowball's	E. ...	2 25
" Plane, Colenso's. Part I., with the use of		
Logarithms, ...	E. ...	1 00
" " Key to above ...	E. ...	1 00
" " Part II., ...	E. ...	1 00
" " " Key to,	E. ...	1 25
" " the two parts bound to-		
gether	E. ...	1 50
" Plane and Spherical, Loomis's ...	A. ...	1 00
" Plane, Perkins'	A. ...	1 50

MORAL PHILOSOPHY AND SCIENCE.

Abercombie's Moral Philosophy, ...	A. ...	0 62½
Cousins' History of Modern Philosophy, translated by Wight,		
2 vols., ...	A. ...	3 00
" Lectures on the True, the Beautiful & the Good,	A. ...	1 50
Gerhart's Philosophy and Logic, ...	A. ...	1 00
Hamilton's (Sir W.) Moral Philosophy	A. ...	1 50
Locke on the Human Understanding, ...	E. ...	1 50
Macintosh's Ethical Philosophy, ...	A. ...	1 00
Morell's History of Philosophy, ...	A. ...	2 75
Newton's Principia, by Whewell, ...	E. ...	0 62½
Paley's Moral and Political Philosophy,... A. 62½.	E. ...	0 75
Pinnock's Catechism of Intellectual Philosophy, ...	E. ...	0 20
Reid's Intellectual Powers. Ed. by Sir W. Hamilton,	A. ...	1 25
" " Ed. by Walker, ...	E. ...	1 25
Reid's Active Powers, by Wright, ...	E. ...	3 00
Schwegler's Epitome of the History of Philosphy,	A. ...	1 25
Stewart's Active and Moral Powers, ...	A. ...	1 25
" " " Edited by Walker,	E. ...	1 37½
" Philosophy of the Human Mind, ...	A. ...	1 50
Wayland's Elements of Modern Science, ...	A. ...	1 25
Winslow's Elements of Modern Philosophy, ...	A. ...	1 25

NATURAL HISTORY.

Conchology, Pinnock's Catechism of	...	E.	... 0 20
Child's Book of Nature. By Hooker. Part II. Animals.	A.	... 0 50
Lessons on the Universe,	...	E.	... 0 60
Natural History, Goldsmith's	...	A.	... 0 75
" Pinnock's Catechism of	...	E.	... 0 20
" Macallum's Chart of	...	Toronto,	1 00
" " " Mounted, &c.	"	... 1 50
Zoology. Agassiz and Gould's Principles of A. $0 75	E.	... 1 00
" Patterson's First Steps,	...	E.	... 0 75
" " Introduction to	...	E.	... 1 50
" Pinnock's Catechism of	...	E.	... 0 20
" Carpenter's	...	E.	... 1 75

NATURAL PHILOSOPHY.

Chambers' Natural Philosophy,... E. 0 90 ... A. ... 0 75
Comstock's System of Natural Philosophy ... A. ... 0 62½
Lardner's Natural Philosophy, 3 vols,, ... A. ... 5 00
MacGauley's Natural Philosophy, ... E. ... 2 50
Olmsted's Compendium of Natural Philosophy, ... A. ... 1 00
Parker's Juvenile Philosophy, ... A. ... 0 20
" First Lessons in Natural Philosophy, ... A. ... 0 30
" Natural and Experimental, ... E. ... 1 00
Paley's Natural Philosophy, ... E. ... 0 75
Pinnock's Catechism of Natural Philosophy, ... E. ... 0 20
Reynolds' Diagrams of Nat. Philosophy, 12 in p. folio. E. ... 3 00
Tomlinson's Introduction to Natural Philosophy, (Weales
  series.) ... ... E. ... 0 30
Wilson's First Lessons in Natural Philosophy, ... E. ... 0 65
" Second " ", ... E. ... 0 20
Acoustics, Chamber's Educational Course, ... E. ... 0 30
Hydrodynamics, Pinnock's Catechism of, ... E. ... 0 20
Hydrostatics and Hydraulics, Chamber's Educational
  Course, ... E. ... 0 25
Electricity, Chamber's Educational Course, ... E. ... 0 30
Magnetism, Davis' Manual of, ... E. ... 1 00
Meteorology, Chamber's Educational Course, ... E. ... 0 30
" Drew's, ... E. ... 1 75
" Brocklesby's, ... A. ... 0 60
Optics, Chamber's Educational Course, ... E. ... 0 30
" Pinnock's Catechism of,... ... E. ... 0 20
Pneumatics, " " ... ... E. ... 0 20
" Tomlinson's, Weales' Series,... ... E. ... 0 30
Hooker's Child's Book of Nature, ... A. ... 0 25
Schoedler and Medlock's Book of Nature, ... A. ... 1 88

PHYSIOLOGY.

			$ Crs.
Beecher, Miss C., Physiology and Calisthenics, ...	A.	...	0 50
Chamber's Rudiments of Animal Physiology,	E.	...	0 30
Comings' Class Book of Physiology, ...	A.	...	0 90
Cutter's First Book of Anatomy, Physiology, &c.,...	A.	...	0 50
" Second Book, " "	A.	...	1 00
Hooker's Human Physiology, Book 1, ...	A.	...	0 50
" " " Book 2, ...	A.	...	1 00
Lambert's First Book of Physiology, ...	A.	...	0 50
" Popular, " ...	A.	...	1 00

RHETORIC.

Blair's Lectures on Rhetoric, ...	A.	...	0 50
Boyd's Elements of Rhetoric, ...	A.	...	0 50
Campbell's Philosophy of Rhetoric, ...	A.	...	1 25
Pinnock's Catechism of Rhetoric, ...	E.	...	0 20
Quackenbos' Elements of Composition and Rhetoric, A.		...	1 00
Whateley's Rhetoric, ...	E.	...	0 88
" " ...	A.	...	0 75

SPELLING BOOKS, PRIMERS, AND READERS.

Butter's Etymological Spelling Book, ...	E.	...	0 45
Canada Spelling, ...	... Toronto,		0 12½
Carpenter's " ...	... Toronto,		0 12½
Cobb's " ...	... Toronto,		0 12½
Davis' Reading made Easy, ...	... Montreal,		0 10
Fennings' Spelling, ...	E.	...	0 20
Introduction to the Art of Reading,	E.	...	0 25
Lennie's Ladder, ...	E.	...	0 30
Mavors's English Spelling, ...	... Toronto,		0 12½
Model Lessons, 3 Vols., ...	E.	...	2 00
Murray's Introduction to English Reading,	... Toronto,		0 20
" " " "	E.	...	0 45
" Reader ...	E.	...	0 80
" Exercises in English Reading,...	E.	...	0 30
" Spelling, ...	E.	...	0 45
McCulloch's Lessons on Prose and Verse	E.	...	0 55
Routledge's Linen Primers, ...	E.	...	0 12½
" " ...	E.	...	0 25
Sullivan's Literary Class Book,...	E.	...	0 62½
" Spelling Book Superseded,	A.	...	0 20
Tegg's First Book, ...	E.	...	0 12½
Webster's Elementary Spelling,,	... Toronto,		0 12½
Webb's Pupils' Guide. ...	A.	...	0 25

				$ Cts.
Trench's Lessons on Proverbs, ...	...	... A.	...	0 62½
Parley's Christian Evidences, ...	...	... E.	...	0 75
" Natural Theology, illustrated, ...	...	... A.	...	1 25
Pinnock's Catechism of Heraldry,	...	... E.	...	0 20
" " Drawing,	...	... E.	...	0 20
" " British Constitution,	...	... E.	...	0 20
" " History of the Jews,	...	... E.	...	0 20
" " Mythology,	...	... E.	...	0 20

SUNDRIES.

SLATES—Hard and Soft Wood Frames.
" Metallic.
" Porcelain.
" Book.
" Reeves' Flexible.

Copy Books—Maclear & Co.'s superior make, Foolscap 4to.
" " Small and large Post 4to.

Ruled Small, Round, or Text Hand.

Swan's Copy Books, with Head Lines, Nos. 1 to 15.

Smith's Copy Slips, twenty-five styles.

DRAWING PENCILS, PAPER, BOOKS. &c

MATHEMATICAL INSTRUMENTS.

BOXES OF COLOURS, INK, STEEL PENS OF THE MOST APPROVED MAKERS, QUILLS, INDIA RUBBER, RULERS,

TOGETHER WITH EVERY REQUISITE FOR SCHOOL PURPOSES, OF THE BEST QUALITIES AND AT THE LOWEST PRICES.